OLD FRIENDS, NEW FRIENDS

By Joanne Ryder

Illustrated by Jane Chambless-Rigie

W9-BMT-022

For my friends, Grace and Mark Koch

A GOLDEN BOOK • NEW YORK
Western Publishing Company, Inc., Racine, Wisconsin 53404

After school, Grace waited by the big oak tree for her best friend, Laura. Laura was trying out for the class play.

"I hope she gets the part," thought Grace.

"I got it," shouted Laura as she ran down the school steps.

"Fantastic," said Grace. "You'll be the best Queen of the Jungle ever."

"Let's go," said Laura, smiling. "I'd better start studying my lines. The play is only three weeks away."

The girls went to Grace's house to practice.

"I have to bring my own costume," Laura said. "What do you think I should wear?"

Grace pulled out a big box. Inside was a present from her favorite uncle.

"You can wear this," she said.

"Oh, it's perfect," said Laura.

At school the next day, Grace carried her lunch tray to her usual table. Another girl was sitting in the seat she always chose.

"Hi, Grace," said Laura. "This is Jean. She's the Mouse Queen in our play."

Grace ate her lunch quietly while the two girls read their parts.

When school was over, Grace waited for Laura at their usual place. But Laura didn't come.

Finally Grace walked home alone.

Grace walked by Laura's house. Laura and Jean were in the back yard.

"I waited for you," Grace told her friend.

"Oh, I forgot," said Laura. "I'm really sorry. We had to hurry home so we could practice."

"Can I help?" asked Grace.

"You can listen," said Jean.

Grace listened, but then she got bored. She turned three cartwheels on the grass—*flop, flippity flop.*

"It's a little noisy here," said Jean.

"I guess I'd better leave," said Grace. She headed for the park.

There were a lot of skaters in the park, and Grace stopped to watch them. She wished she had brought her new roller skates.

"I wish Laura were here, too," she thought.

The next day Grace asked Laura to go skating after school.

"Jean and I have to practice," said Laura.

"You spend all your time with her," said Grace.

"You're being mean," said Laura. "You don't like Jean because she's my friend."

"I thought you were *my* friend," said Grace.

"I am," said Laura, "but you're being silly."

So Grace went to the park by herself. She skated by the pond. Then she tried to skate backward, but she fell down.

"You turned too fast," she heard someone say. It was Pete, a boy in her music class. He skated backward down the path toward her.

"I wish I could skate like you," said Grace.

"You just need practice," said Pete. "Meet me tomorrow, and I'll teach you."

Every day after school, Grace and Pete skated together. After a few weeks of practice, Grace skated much better.

"We should enter the skating contest tomorrow," Pete said. "You could be my partner."

"Okay!" said Grace.

Every day after school, Laura and Jean practiced for
the play.

"I'm scared," said Jean. "The play is tomorrow night."

"I'm scared, too," said Laura. "Let's not practice
anymore today. I think we need a break."

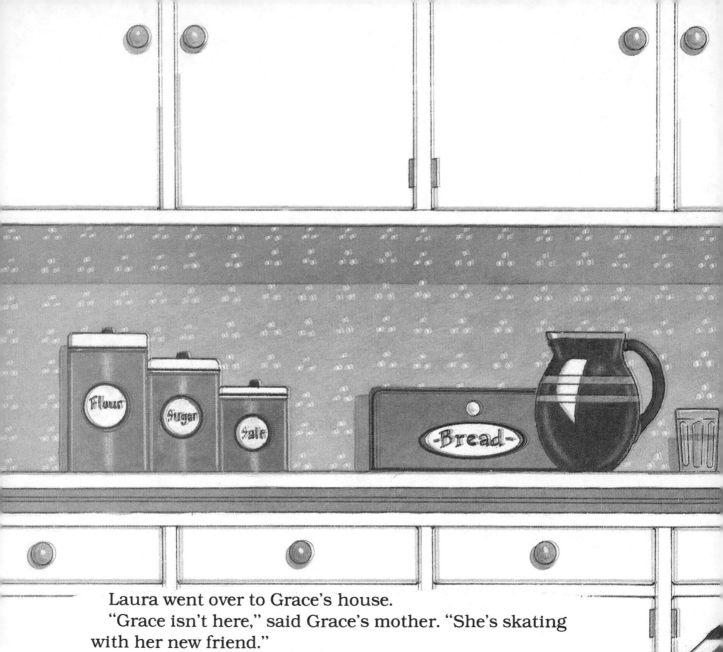

Laura went over to Grace's house.

"Grace isn't here," said Grace's mother. "She's skating with her new friend."

"Oh," said Laura. "I wanted to invite her to my house after the play. We're having cake and ice cream."

"I'll tell her," said Grace's mother.

Then Laura said softly, "She can bring her friend if she likes."

The park was very crowded for the skating contest.
Pete and Grace did some fancy tricks and the crowd
cheered.

Grace heard somebody cheering very loudly. It was
Laura.

Pete and Grace won second prize. After the judge gave
them their red ribbons, Grace looked for Laura. But
Laura was gone.

That evening Grace went to the play early. She sat in the first row and saved a seat for Pete.

The play was a hit. Laura knew all her lines. When she sang her big song, she looked right at Grace.

At the end of the play, Grace clapped and clapped. Then she and Pete went to Laura's house.

"Welcome to the party," said Laura's mother. "I hear you two were big winners today."

Pete and Grace smiled at her.

"You were wonderful," Pete told Laura.

"You were great, too," Grace told Jean.

Laura's mother made ice-cream sundaes. Pete did some magic tricks and Jean told a lot of funny jokes. Everyone had a good time.

After their friends left, Laura gave Grace her costume.

"Pete is nice," said Laura.

"Jean is nice, too," said Grace.

"Jean is my friend," said Laura, "but you are my best friend."

"And you are mine," said Grace.

The next morning Laura waited for Grace, and they walked to school together. They ate lunch together and stood together in music class.

And after school, they went to Laura's yard and played their favorite games together. Just the two best friends.